Trickster Tales from Prairie Lodgefires

As told to Bernice G. Anderson
by Ingaglueh-Whoo-Tongah of the Poncas
and by Maunkee Blackbear Tahbone of the Kiowas

Trickster Tales from Prairie Lodgefires

Collected by

Bernice G. Anderson

illustrated by Frank Gee

Abingdon
Nashville

In memory of my husband Lyle Anderson
to whom Grandma Maunkee of the Kiowas gave the
name PAH-SOTI-THI, White Thunder

Contents

Trickster Tales from Prairie Lodgefires

Trickster

In the Far Back Times, tribes about the western prairies told and retold how-things-came-to-be tales around their lodgefires. They held storytelling sessions at their own tribal powwows and also at intertribal powwows. Even in these modern times, at intertribal powwows, they still have storytelling periods which sometimes occur during daylight hours. But one kind of story is never, never told in daytime, but always at night. Such stories are about the character who was half Medicine Man, half Trickster. (You never knew whether he would be in a mood to do good or to trick you!)

When Trickster was about to leave our world, he commanded the people never to tell stories about him in daytime, so that is the way it has been, to this very day, wherever Trickster tales are told.

All tribes that live around the prairies have a Trickster character. Each tribe has its own name for him, but the deeds and misdeeds of the Trickster reported by one tribe are so similar to those told by another tribe that there is no doubt he is the same fellow. A constant traveler, he was likely to appear in any tribe's camp at any time.

No one actually knows in which tribe any of the following Trickster tales originated. Told and retold by storytellers at intertribal gatherings, the goings-on of "Old Man Napi" of the Blackfoot tribe, "Old Man Coyote" of the Crow tribe, "Uncle Sainday" of the Kiowas, "Grandfather Iktoemi," of the Dakotas or Sioux, "Old Man Wihio" of the Cheyennes, or Trickster whatever-the-name of another tribe. Every person told the version of each Trickster tale that he liked best and let the matter of its origin go at that.

Most descriptions of Trickster by whatever name are the same. He was tall, lanky, and ungainly. His thinning hair was black and coarse and hung like a frayed rope on his bony shoulders. His huge nose had the appearance of standing out in front of his face to point the way in which he should travel.

Animals and people knew him well. Insects knew him too, and so did plants, trees, sun, moon, and stars. The wind, as it journeyed from sky to earth and across the plains, hills, and valleys, often paused and fanned Trickster's perspiring brow as it piped in a whiney voice, "Good day to you, Uncle!" or "Good day to you, Old Man" or whatever the name he was going by. And Trickster always answered in the wind's tone of voice— sometimes high-pitched, sometimes low, and sometimes broken in the middle like the voice of a boy about to become a man. Trickster was proud that he had learned to speak like the wind.

All people and things of the earth and sky knew Trickster, and Trickster not only understood and spoke the language of people, but of all birds and animals as well. He spoke tree-language also and held long conversations with talkative brooks in the valleys and with streams found among towering blue-in-the-distance mountains. He often talked with flowers that blossomed along the prairie and mountain trails. But, whether he stopped to talk or whether he kept on moving, everyone knew when Trickster was coming along. That's what they always said about him, "Trickster is coming along!"

He was very old; no one knew how old, not even Trickster himself. Usually people and all living creatures liked him. Usually, too, everyone was suspicious of him for he was known everywhere as a prankster and cheater. However, when occasion arose, he could be, and often was, a helper and a healer. He had wonderful Medicine Power when he chose to use it, and this explains why he had so many friends. No one knew what to expect of him, though, so sooner or later everyone he met was fooled by him in one way or another.

Being able to turn himself into an animal or bird whenever he chose was one of his accomplishments. He could cause trees and bushes to do amazing things, a trick which he often performed. But occasionally his tricks backfired. At such times everyone had a good laugh at his expense and enjoyed telling about it when groups sat around the lodgefires on winter nights or under the stars in summer.

The following Kiowa Trickster Tales are given here as they were related to me by Grandmother Maunkee (Doing with the Hands) or Alice Blackbear Tahbone of the Kiowas who heard them and told them herself around the Kiowa lodgefires all the years of her life. When she allowed me to record the tales she spoke in the Kiowa tongue, simultaneously shaping her words in sign talk. By watching carefully I could catch some of what she was saying, because I had been taught many of the signs. But her gestures were too rapid for me to keep up with her. When she had finished each tale, her son F. Blackbear Bosin, Sr. translated her spoken words into English. Grandmother's English was as faltering as my Kiowa.

The Trickster Tales of the other tribes were told to me by Ingaglueh-Whoo-Tongah (Roaring Thunder) or Louis McDonald of the Poncas, who had heard them many times around Ponca lodgefires and at intertribal powwows.

Napi's Wager
with Rabbit

Old Man Napi was lying flat on his back, one night, on his bed of buffalo robes. He was gazing up the tepee's smokehole and wishing he could go to sleep. From the position of the stars he could tell the time was halfway between midnight and daybreak. It was not a time when anyone should be lying awake, even though the stars were like a bouquet of flowers, and a brown thrasher was

16

singing a soft voiced song in a nearby cottonwood tree. This had been a longer night than usual; Old Man Napi had come in as soon as Dark had dropped his blanket over Earth and owls began flying about. None of his people wanted to stay outdoors when owls were flying about and hooting because it meant unhappiness and danger.

Old Man was still open-eyed when Sun Chief arose from his lodge in the east and painted himself. So he too arose and went down to the clean little stream that chattered along the side of his camp. There he bathed himself, rubbing his body briskly. He used a pronged stick to comb his tangled, ropelike hair. No one was there to notice whether he combed it or not. However, he was about to take off on one of his journeys, and someone might possibly happen along to tell him goodbye. Of course, someone did, too. While he was pulling on his moccasins, Rabbit came hopping along.

"Good morning, Old Man!" Rabbit called cheerily. "Did you have a restful night before starting on your journey?" That was not the most tactful remark Rabbit could have made; he knew very well that Old Man was a poor sleeper.

Old Man crossly replied, "No, Friend Rabbit, I did not have a restful night. I didn't sleep a wink."

Rabbit clicked his tongue. "To tell you the truth, Napi, I had a wretched night myself. It is as hard for me to sleep as it is for you." He lifted his left hind

leg and scratched his left ear. "But I'll make a wager with you that I can go to sleep and wake up before you do. The one who loses the wager will have to furnish breakfast for the other." Rabbit sat scratching himself while he waited for Napi to reply.

"That will be an easy way for me to get a free breakfast," Old Man Napi said with a dry cackle.

"That's what you think!" said Rabbit.

"What did you say?" Napi asked sharply.

"I said let's start to blink. Blink our eyes, you know. Are you sleepy enough to start going to sleep right away?"

Napi sputtered as if he had tried to swallow a big mouthful of water and choked on it—"Certainly, I'm sleepy enough! Didn't I tell you I didn't sleep a wink all night?" But he was thinking at the same time that he would only pretend to be asleep. He leaned against a tree and closed his eyes to give the impression that he could not remain awake another moment. Rabbit had leaned against another tree.

Every little while Napi opened one eye—just a slit—to see if Rabbit had gone to sleep. But every time Napi looked he noticed that Rabbit's eyes were still open. So Napi decided that he would have plenty of time to take a real nap and still wake up before Rabbit did. He had forgotten that rabbits sleep with their eyes open!

Rabbit had dropped off to sleep right away. He had told the truth when he said that he had not rested well during the night. Rabbit thought he

19

knew Old Man Napi very well, and he did. Napi not only dropped off for a short nap; he was having a deep sleep and was snoring noisily.

A squirrel crept up and sat watching the sleeping Napi curiously. A lizard slithered through the grass and across his feet without waking him. A rising wind tiptoed across the grass and ruffled the eagle feather fastened in Old Man's hair; it made dimples in Rabbit's fur and ran its fingers over the leafy shrubs on the creek bank. Sun Chief climbed higher and higher in the sky and finally shone down on the tree trunk where Rabbit had been leaning. Then it crept over Napi's face and awakened him. He jumped quickly to his feet, groaning, "Oh no, no, no! I meant only to take a short nap! And where is that rabbit?"

Napi stumbled up the bank to his tepee. Just as he feared, his food was gone. The sly rabbit had won his wager; no doubt of that.

Why Rabbits Have
Only a Little Fat

During a long ago Snow-Time Napi was traveling over the plains. As far as he could see, the undulating prairie lay before him, and the wind on the grass made the land look like brown-green water flowing into the horizon. The weather was not yet cold enough to snow, but there was a nippiness in the air, and he wanted to get back to his mountain home before winter settled in.

No other person was in sight. Napi was lonesome and hungry. Antelopes dashed across the prairie with the speed of arrows; rabbits jumped up from hidden hollows and lopped rapidly away; bevies of quail whirred suddenly up from bunches of grass. All were too quick for Napi. He couldn't catch any of them to satisfy his hunger.

Abruptly he came upon a pack of wolves. The grandfather, their chief, was sitting in the exact center of a circle that looked like a Council Meeting.

Napi sidled up to the group. "Pity me, Wolf Chief!" he whined. "Make me one of you that I may have plenty of company and learn your knack for catching rabbits and antelope and everything else that's fleet of foot."

Being in a good mood Wolf Chief said, "All right, come here and let me rub your body with my paws to make long hair immediately grow all over you."

Napi stammered, "N-not hair all over my body! Only on my bald head and arms, I beg of you!"

Wolf Chief didn't see why Napi objected to being made to look like a wolf since he wanted to be like one, but he good-naturedly rubbed only his head and arms and legs. Then he gave Napi three wolves for companions. One was a swift runner; one a fairly good runner; and one a slow runner, but full of cunning. "Go now, and learn how to hunt," he said. Napi and the three wolf companions hunted by day and slept at night or hunted by night and slept by day, whichever they felt like doing. Whenever they lay down to sleep the wolves crowded around Old Man Napi and covered him with their bushy tails to keep him warm.

One sun after Napi and the three wolves started hunting together, they saw a herd of deer. Chasing them they managed to kill four. Napi really didn't do anything, he just pretended to. When they were about to eat the tender, juicy meat, Wolf Chief and the rest of his pack came along and suggested that they make pemmican of the meat so there would be enough for all of them to eat. One of the wolves brought berries to pound into the meat, and the pemmican-maker of the pack started to work. Before he began he said, "All of you must close your eyes. I don't want any of you watching me while I work."

Napi soon opened his eyes—just a crack—and the pemmican-maker saw him. "I told you not to watch me!" he snarled and angrily aimed a round bone at Napi, hitting him on the nose.

"Eeow! That hurt," Napi said. "Let me make the pemmican." The pemmican-maker didn't think Napi could. So, just to show him up, he turned the job over to Napi and sat down.

Napi told all the wolves to close their eyes, as before. Then he started to work. But, in about the time it took to take a long breath, he stopped pounding and threw a bone—hard—at the wolf that had hit him. It struck the wolf with such force it killed him. Wolf Chief became very angry at Napi. "You have killed your brother!" he said. "Now you can't live with us any longer. Take one of your present companions, and the two of you go off to hunt by yourselves."

Having been made one of the wolf pack, Napi was subject to the chief's rules. He chose Swift Runner as his companion. Swift Runner wasn't happy about this, but he, too, was subject to the rules laid down by the chief. So the two outcasts went off to live by themselves.

They managed to kill all the antelope, deer, rabbits, and quail they could eat. But one night Napi had a strange dream. When he awoke at dawn he said to Swift Runner, "I've had a vision and have been told to warn you about something."

"What is it that you must warn me about?"

"It's this. From now on, whenever you chase after something while hunting, if it jumps over water you must not follow it. Never jump over any water. That will be reason for sorrow."

Swift Runner was careful for a long time. But one day a deer that he had been chasing jumped over a stream of water surrounding a wooded island. Without thinking of the warning Swift Runner jumped over the water and landed on the island. But the moment he entered the timber on the island a bear jumped out of a thicket and caught him. The island was the home of Bear Chief and his three brothers.

Napi waited long and long for Swift Runner to return. Finally when he decided that his companion was never coming back he set out to look for him. He called to a rabbit that was lopping by, "Have you seen my brother wolf?"

"No!" the rabbit replied, "And if I never see him it will not be too long! Wolves are cruel to rabbits. I hear too that you are not only cruel to rabbits, you're cruel to your brother wolves whenever you feel like it."

"Hi-yah!" exclaimed quick-tempered Napi, "You are an impudent rabbit. I'll punish you and all the rabbit tribe if I ever get another chance!" But Rabbit only laughed and lopped away.

Napi asked the birds he met if they had seen his brother wolf, but the birds knew him as no friend of theirs. They merely flew away.

Finally he saw a kingfisher sitting on a weeping willow tree that dripped its leafy tears into the water. Kingfisher was peering intently down at the clear, running stream. He did not look up when Napi asked of him, "Are you looking for something, or merely admiring your reflection in that water-mirror?"

"Don't jest," Kingfisher retorted, still not looking up. "Bear Chief has killed your wolf brother. He and his brother bears have eaten the meat and thrown the fat into this stream. Whenever I see some floating along I dart down to get it."

Napi became very angry and excited inside

himself, although on the outside he looked exactly the same. At least Kingfisher didn't notice any difference in his tone of voice when Napi asked, "Where does Bear Chief live?"

"He lives in the timber on the island. He and his three brothers come down to the shore opposite here every morning to bathe."

Old Man Napi hung around until Kingfisher had flown away. Then he crossed the stream and went to the place he had been told was the bears' bathing beach. He changed himself into a hollow tree and waited.

At sunrise the next day Bear Chief and his brothers ambled down to the bank of the stream. They noticed the hollow tree at once. "Look!" shouted the chief, "That tree has not been here before. It is Napi. I know his tricks! Go, Brothers, claw the tree to see if I am right."

The brothers clawed the tree long and hard. Old Man Napi winced inside himself, but he didn't move a muscle. The brothers reported that it was indeed a tree. But Bear Chief was not convinced.

"It has never been there before," Bear Chief said. "Trees don't grow that size and then become hollow overnight!" He went over to it himself and clawed and bit the tree until Napi could stand it no longer. However, just as he was about to open his mouth to yell, Bear Chief turned away satisfied. "If that had been Napi," he remarked, "he couldn't have kept from yelping. I know that fellow very well."

"That's what you think!" Napi wanted to say, but he remained motionless until the bears had turned their backs and started into the water for their bath. Then Napi leaned over and shot an arrow into the hind-end of each of them. Now the bears were the ones who yelped. They let out noises like loud claps of thunder as they tore back into the timber. The feathered ends of the arrows were sticking out of their rumps like the tails of some grotesque tribe of birds.

Napi doubled up with laughter as he changed himself back into his true self. Walking along the bank he came to a place where a large green frog was exercising himself by diving from the bank into the stream, then leaping back in order to dive again. He was croaking as he jumped. Drawing near Napi realized that the frog was not merely croaking, he was singing a song in the Blackfoot language:

> "O-kyai-yu . . . O-kyai-yu . . .
>   Napi I-nit-si-wah!"
> "Bear Chief . . . Bear Chief . . .
>   Old Man Napi killed him!"

Napi did not know that anyone had seen him shoot the arrows into the bears. He was not sure he liked the idea, either, for no telling what might happen to him before he could get away from the island. Besides how could he be sure he had really

killed the chief of the bears? He decided he had better stop to do some thinking. So he sat down and covered his head with his robe.

Soon he got up, having changed his face so that Frog would not recognize him. Then he walked over to Frog and called, "Good day, friend!" Frog was so startled at hearing a voice close to him that he turned a somersault backwards instead of diving forward into the water. Then he saw the person belonging to the voice, and he sat there staring with big, bulgy eyes.

"Did I hear you say something about Bear Chief being dead?" asked Napi.

"Yes! Old Man Napi shot him and his three brothers. The arrows are still sticking in their rumps like feathered spears."

"Or like bird tails, maybe?" Napi tried not to smile.

"Not like any bird tails I ever saw," said Frog. "They really aren't dead yet. But if anyone should happen to hit the arrows, even slightly, some vital spot might be pierced, and the bears would surely die."

Napi clicked his tongue in pretended pity. "Too bad! Too bad!" he murmured.

"Oh, not *too* bad," Frog said. "I am getting ready now to go cure them through my Medicine Power."

"This will never do!" Old Man said quickly. Too quickly.

"What was that you said?" demanded Frog.

"I—I said—what a fine thing to do!" stammered Napi. Because Frog was looking suspicious, he knew he must act quickly. So he grabbed Frog and killed him. Then he carefully removed Frog's skin and stretched it until it fit his own body. Then, with much effort and many hops Napi managed to reach the place where the bears lay groaning. He hopped toward them, croaking Frog's Medicine Song. "O-kyai-yu . . . O-kyai-yu . . . Nih-nah . . ." he began, but he didn't know the medicine part of the song so he mumbled some words that didn't mean anything. Bear Chief was puzzled, but he was hurting so much he didn't try to understand. He knew Frog had sent word that he was coming to cure him and his brothers, and he wanted him to get busy. "Hurry up with your medicine!" he roared at the frog who was Napi. So Napi hopped close to him and quickly shoved the entire arrow into his body while he murmured in his ear, "There's the kind of medicine you deserve for killing my brother wolf." Bear Chief fell over, dead.

"A-ha! I cured him!" croaked Napi aloud. "He has fallen asleep." And he hopped very close to the biggest of the brothers. "Here is your medicine," he croaked. And he gave the same "medicine" to the other bears. Then he skinned all four bears and built a big fire over which to render the fat and to roast the meat.

After the fat had been rendered, he poured it into

a hollow he had made in the ground. Then he lifted his true voice to summon all the animals that lived on the island. Soon the deer, the antelope, the elk, the coyotes, the rabbits and the other animals came running to see what the excitement was about.

"Now," said Napi, "here is fat for you to roll in so that from now on you may be fat instead of so skinny."

Bears that had been living on the other side of the island were the first to rush up and wallow in the big basin of fat. That is why all bears are fat to this day. The rabbits tried next, but Old Man Napi put out his hand to stop them. "Na-na!" he said. "I told a rabbit who was saucy to me that I would punish him and all his tribe if I ever got a chance. Now you are to wait until all the other animals have rolled in the fat. If there's any left after that, you may have it."

When the bears were finished, the animals took turns rolling in the fat. Finally the rabbits were allowed to take their turn. Very little was left in the hollow by that time. But the rabbits filled their paws with what grease they could scrape up and rubbed it on their backs and between their hind legs.

This is the reason today's rabbits have only two layers of fat—on their backs and between their hind legs. It was all Old Man Napi's doing.

Why the Bob-Cat Stays in the Woods

Trickster Sainday was coming along. And he was hungry; he was seldom without a gnawing in his stomach. Whenever his huge nose caught a whiff of something cooking or his eyes caught sight of anything that looked like food, his giant feet walked his lanky body right there. That is how it happened that Sainday was at the twist of the trail on a certain hillside when a meatball came rolling along like a fair-sized snowball.

After the meatball came a ball of hackberries; after the hackberries came a ball of black haws from the hawthorn tree.

The meatball saw Sainday drooling at the mouth like a hungry coyote. "You poor, hungry fellow!" she said. "Take a bite out of my round, fat side. I can spare a little for you." Sainday took a big bite of the juicy meatball. And the meatball moved slowly along.

The hackberry ball said, "You may take a bite out of my side too. Everyone likes my little round berries. Rolled into a ball like this they are very tasty, so help yourself!" Sainday did. Then along came the ball of black haws. She said, "You still look hungry, poor fellow! Take a bite out of my side, too!"

But Sainday still wasn't satisfied; his stomach seemed without a bottom. After the hawthorn ball had moved slowly along, he jumped up and ran through vines and thickets and over large rocks until he came to where the trail twisted around the hill. He was just in time, too, for here came the meatball, the hackberry ball, and the black haw ball on their journey down to the valley.

Sainday took off his beaded headband to make himself look different—like an entirely new person, he hoped. The trick worked! When the meatball saw him she exclaimed, "You poor, hungry looking man! Take a bite out of me before I roll on down the hill to the valley!" So Sainday took a second bite of the juicy meatball. The hackberry and hawthorn balls told him to take bites out of their sides also. But as they rolled on down the winding trail, greedy Sainday was still hungry. He cut across more vines and thickets and large rocks until he reached the next bend in the twisting trail.

Sainday was out of breath, but he managed to get there before the three rolling balls. This time he took off his hunting jacket so he would look like a still different person. Then he stretched his lanky frame down beside the trail and pretended to sleep.

The meatball stopped and nudged him on the nose. His nose itched in his effort to keep from sniffing too eagerly that appetizing aroma. Sitting up, he rubbed his eyes in pretended bewilderment. "Who are you?" he asked.

"I am Meat Ball, and these are my friends, Hackberry Ball and Hawthorn Ball. We are travelers on our way to the valley."

"I, too am on my way to the valley," said Sainday. "But I am too weak from hunger to go much farther."

"This hill seems to be full of hungry old men!" said Meat Ball. "Take a bite of me before I roll on. I am plumper than I need to be."

"Take a bite of me, too!" said Hackberry Ball.

"And of me, too," said Hawthorn Ball.

Trickster Sainday gulped down his third big helping of food. Then he called after the departing balls: "You'll find another hungry man on down the hill a way." Then he made haste to see that he did not make a liar out of himself—this time, at least.

Sure enough, as the balls rounded the last curve in the twisted alligator tail of a trail, there was a man waiting. This time when Sainday opened his mouth to take a bite of the meatball, the three balls noticed a piece of black haw that had become stuck between his two front teeth and recognized him.

Hurt and disgusted the three balls jerked themselves out of Sainday's reach and rolled swiftly down the hill and into a creek to get away from him.

Not to be outdone, Sainday rushed down and built a fire on the bank of the creek. He put stones into it and heated them red hot. Using a forked stick he heaved the hot stones one by one into the creek where the balls lay. The stones heated the water and made soup out of the three balls. Sainday was sure the soup would be delicious, but just as he was about to dip up a bowl full of it, using big clam shells that lay on the bank, Kapogeh, the coyote came by.

"Give me some of your soup, Uncle!" Coyote begged.

"Na-na!" Sainday replied. "There's not enough for two such hungry fellows as you and I are!"

With that Sainday turned his back on Coyote and hurriedly began to dip up the soup with his bare hands. But the stones had made the soup so hot that he dropped the clam-shell bowls, and they broke. So he ran along the bank in search of another bowl and something he could use for a spoon. His quest took him around the bend of the creek, and that was his big mistake!

When he was out of sight, Bob-Cat, who didn't mind the heat, dipped his big paws into the creek and tasted the soup. Ummm was it good! He looked once more in the direction that Sainday had disappeared then waded into the creek and lapped it dry.

When he had had his fill, he leaped up the bank and disappeared into the woods where purple shadows pattern the ground.

Sainday was furious when he returned with a large shell for a dish and a small shell for a spoon but nothing to use them for. He knew, of course, who the guilty one was. There were greasy tracks leading into the woods.

Sainday found the tricky bob-cat asleep in a purple splatter of shadows that made him look almost like the shadows themselves. Bob-cat was so full of soup he was in a stupor and did not feel a thing when Sainday took a sharp rock and filed his long nose down to a mere stub.

Now Sainday, shaking Bob-Cat awake, suggested

the two of them go over to a puddle of rainwater at the edge of the woods to look at themselves.

Stumbling along like a sleepwalker Bob-Cat went with Sainday, but he woke in a hurry when he saw himself with his long nose cut off. His reflection frightened him so that he shot back into the woods and ever since, has been ashamed to come out in the daytime. He had lost his tail long, long ago, and now he possessed a snub nose.

Bob-Cat never wanted to see his face again, or be seen by anyone. But sometimes in the night, he can be heard wailing about the trick Sainday played on him.

How Sainday
Brought the Buffalo

At a certain Long-Ago Time the people could not find any buffalo herds when they went hunting. There was hunger and a need for buffalo hides for tepees, clothing, and bedding.

One day Sainday was coming along on one of his endless journeys. When he saw how hungry and cold his people were and that the children were taking no interest in their games, but just sitting around shivering, he knew he must get busy and do something to help them. Sainday did have pity in his heart, sometimes.

Being a Medicine Man as well as Trickster, Sainday sensed that something out of the ordinary was wrong. It was true they were having cold weather earlier this year, but it was still autumn. The grass was green, and the waterholes on the prairie were full. Something strange was going on. Sainday kept his eyes and ears open while he continued to call upon his Power to help him find the reason for the disappearance of the buffalo.

One day as he was coming along his attention was drawn to a litle girl playing under a lone cottonwood tree at the edge of the village. What he noticed, especially, was that she was playing—all the other children of the village were too listless to move. Next he observed that the girl's body was plump, and her eyes sparkled. "Ummm!" thought Sainday. "There is something queer about this! I should find out where this child lives." Sainday watched the little girl and discovered that she and her parents lived just beyond the village not far from the cottonwood tree. He learned, too, that they did not mingle with the other people of the tribe and never invited anyone to their home.

There was much to know. The child's father, a bird-man named Mah-Saw-Tih, or White Crow, had ordered his wife to keep a close watch over their daughter; she was not to play with any of the village children nor wander far from home.

The villagers did not like White Crow's aloofness, nor the expression in his cold eyes. No one tried to make friends, which did not displease White Crow for his heart held a secret he did not want anyone to discover.

Because Crow Man noticed the head chief of the tribe looking at him with questions in his eyes, Crow Man told his wife one sun he was going hunting with other men of the tribe. "They don't like me," he said, "but they will not object to my going along."

"But why do you bother to go hunting when we have all the meat we can eat?" his wife asked.

This made Crow Man look around quickly to see if anyone had been near enough to overhear. He cautioned his wife to guard her tongue and whispered, "I go on hunting trips to throw off any doubt the others may have of me. Goodbye, now! Keep our child close to the lodge while I am away." Then he half-flew, half-walked to join the hunting party.

When Sainday saw White Crow among the hunters he said to himself, "This is the chance I've been waiting for!" He changed himself into a small dog and scampered to where the Crow child was playing.

Upon seeing the puppy the Crow girl ran and

gathered it into her arms. "Oh, Mother!" she called, "See! I've found a playmate!"

When Crow Man came in from another meatless hunt and saw the puppy, he ordered his daughter to get rid of it. He, too, possessed medicine power, and knowing Sainday's reputation for trickery, he sensed right away that it might not be a real dog. But his daughter begged so hard, that White Crow finally agreed to let her keep the puppy if she would never take it into the tepee.

Being told not to do something always made the little Crow girl want to do it. The next time her father went hunting and her mother had gone to the creek for water she carried the puppy into the tepee. This was what Sainday had been hoping for. He was sure the secret of NO BUFFALO was to be found in White Crow's lodge.

The first thing Sainday noticed was the fireplace. As all lodge fires are, it was in the center of the tepee, but instead of building the fire on the ground as other women did, White Crow Woman had been building it on a slab of rock which could be seen through the scattered ashes. "Why all this?" asked Sainday of himself. He did not have to wait long to learn the answer. The little White Crow girl ran over and tugged at the slab until she managed to pull it aside.

Sainday-the-puppy peered down into the dark hole she had uncovered and saw that it was an entrance to a tunnel. But before he had taken more than a glance the girl picked him up and held him over the edge. "See, Puppy," she said, "this tunnel leads to where we keep our buffalo and other animals. We have all the fresh meat we want. We don't have to go hungry, as other people do."

Sainday acted as if he were afraid of falling into the hole. This amused the Crow girl, and she laughed gleefully and began to tease Sainday-the-puppy by pretending to drop him. He trembled and wiggled and after a time squirmed around so that he could jump out of her arms and land on his feet. Before she could catch him, he scrambled down into the tunnel.

"Oh, Mother! Mother!" she screamed, as White Crow Woman came in with the jars of water from the creek. "My puppy jumped into the big tunnel!"

Crow Woman hastily set her jars on the floor and ran to the uncovered hole. As she started to scold her daughter for disobeying, they heard a rumbling sound like thunder under the ground. The woman knew it was the thundering of hundreds and hundreds of hoofs. "Run! Run!" she screamed. "Get out of the way or we will be trampled underfoot by the buffalo!"

Sainday-the-puppy had found the buffalo and was driving them out: big ones, fat ones, lean ones, young ones, old ones. "No wonder the hunters have been returning empty-handed!" he muttered. "No wonder people were crying for food and old people were starving." In buffalo language—for

43

Sainday could speak the language of every creature—he shouted, "Go up through the tunnel. Scatter out! Scatter to the four winds!"

He found elk, deer, antelope, rabbits, and fowl too. "Scatter to the four winds—all of you!" he shouted in their own languages. They knew Sainday's voice, and they obeyed.

Sainday knew White Crow Man would be in a rage when he saw the buffalo herds clambering out of his tunnel and fanning out across the plains. And he was sure the selfish fellow would know where to put the blame. Sainday had to do some fast thinking to save himself from Crow Man's own medicine power.

When the buffalo began reappearing on the trails overgrown with grass, White Crow knew his suspicions had been right. "That puppy was Sainday! I knew it! Knew it!" he croaked angrily in his throat as he mounted the air, being half man, half crow. He flew like the wind back to where his tepee had stood. "I'll fix Sainday for this! He must be down there yet for the buffalo and other animals are still pouring out of the tunnel!"

The hunters were grateful to Sainday. They knew it was he who had brought back the buffalo. They had missed him, but they knew, now, what he had been doing. They quickly shot enough buffalo to feed their hungry families and returned to the village where the women were talking excitedly about what was happening north of the village.

"Look!" They pointed with their chins, as all Kiowas do. "There seems to be no end to the herds!"

"There will be an end," said the hunters, "and that's where Sainday will be!" They were right. Sainday was at the end of the herds. But it would be the end of Sainday, too, if he did not think of a way to save himself.

When Mah-Saw-Tih, White Crow, reached the opening of the tunnel he put an arrow in his bow and waited for Sainday to come out either as himself or in the form of the puppy. But Sainday changed himself into a cockleburr and hid in the thick, matted hair of the last buffalo to come out of the tunnel.

Out over the plains this old buffalo went to join his brothers. And Sainday went along, as a cockleburr in the matted hair near his hind hoof—leaving White Crow Man behind. All day and all night White Crow waited beside the hole in the ground, his bow and arrow aimed at the opening.

That was a *good* trick Sainday played this time!

Sainday and Whirlwind Maiden

Sainday was coming along in Pi-gih, Hot-Sun-Weather. He paused along the dusty trail to wipe sweat from his brow and kneel on one bony knee beside a river to dip his broad hand in for a drink. The water at the big bend of the river was always clean and mirror-clear. Sainday liked to look at himself down there and listen to the river talking to itself. This time he decided to lie down for a brief rest.

The chatter of the birds in the tree above Sainday and the river-talk were company for him because he could understand and speak their language. Lying there he fell asleep. But soon he was awakened by a swishing and whirling, swishing and whirling sound. Sitting up, he felt as if his head were whirling too. Then he saw the cause of it all: a tall, slim maiden with unbound hair that reached down to the ground was swishing and whirling about.

The maiden was having such a good time dancing that Sainday thought he would like to join her in her strange dance. Because he didn't know her name, he called, "Good day to you, lively maiden! What is your name and where are you going?"

"My name is Whirlwind. I am going nowhere in particular, only dancing about and stirring up dust to make folk like you ask questions."

"Will you teach me to dance like that? I'd like to whirl along with you wherever you go. I get lonesome always traveling alone."

"Oh, you couldn't do this dance without holding onto me all the time," she answered. "Only whirlwinds can travel in this manner."

"Well, that is all right. I think I would enjoy

traveling by air; my feet get tired of walking all the time."

"Very well, then; it shall be as you ask," said the Whirlwind Maiden with a funny kind of laugh. "Take hold of my sash and hang on tight!"

Sainday did. And soon they were going up . . . up . . . up into the air. They whirled round and round in a cloud of trail dust and swirling leaves, stirring up more dust and more leaves. Yes, Sainday was coming along, he was coming along with the Whirlwind Maiden, Ma-Toy-Gah-Mah. She was never still for a moment except when she took a brief rest on a cloud-bed. Then, because there wasn't room for Sainday, he had to dangle there, holding on as best he could until Whirlwind was ready to start out again.

Never had Sainday imagined such an experience. Traveling with Whirlwind wasn't nearly the fun he had expected it to be. For one thing, Whirlwind sometimes dipped so low Sainday scraped treetops and got scratched by thorns and jagged branches. Often they missed a ragged cliff by mere inches.

Sainday found it harder and harder to hold on to Whirlwind. Finally he quit trying and fell with a thud to the ground. As he landed he was sure he heard Whirlwind give a faint swish of laughter. Rubbing his bruises and putting herbs on his scratches, he said aloud: "Never again will I ask to

travel by air! From now on my feet will take me wherever I want to go." With a sigh of relief he watched Whirlwind dance a zigzag pattern across the prairie and out of sight around the End-of-the-Mountains.

Why All Prairie Dogs Are Brown

Sainday was coming along. His giant feet knew every trail on the prairies and in hill and mountain country. Suntime after suntime he wandered about looking for animals or birds to talk with, to play tricks on, or to help—whatever whim seized him. What an appetite all that walking gave Sainday.

One sun, Sainday came to a prairie-dog village. Prairie dogs of every color were scampering about, diving in and out of their holes or sitting on their mounds and wagging their tails back and forth while they chattered to one another in their own language: "Tdek-ko! Tdek-ko!" Some were black and white, some red, some brown, some yellow. There were prairie dogs of every color of the rainbow.

Seeing how fat the little prairie dogs were, Sainday called out, "Good day to you, nephews! I feel like singing for you. Come over to this open space and dance to my singing!"

Delighted at an invitation to dance the prairie dogs scampered in a group over to the place Sainday had indicated. As they formed a ring around him, Trickster exclaimed, "Oh! I need a drumstick for beating out the rhythm. Wait here, nephews. Wait here, nieces. I'll go cut a drumstick from that dogwood tree by the creek. The ground shall be my tom-tom."

While the prairie dogs eagerly waited on the dance ground, Sainday went to the tree and broke off a branch.

On his way back to the dance ground out of sight of the prairie dogs, he stopped at each hole in the village to clog up the entrance. His sharp eyes missed only one hole.

When he reached the waiting dancers he called out, "Now nephews, now nieces, close your eyes! If you keep your eyes open you'll get a terrible headache." So the prairie dogs tightly closed their eyes. Then Sainday began to sing in the Kiowa tongue:

> "Tsai-gah . . . Tsai-gah,
> Tone ba-toe-tay
> Bah-tone toe-tay
> Oeh-nah bah-low sa!"

> "Prairie-dog . . . prairie-dog
> Shake your tail!
> Keep shaking your tail
> While I make you this song!"

> "Tdek-ko! Tdek-ko!
> Tdek-ko! Tdek-ko!"

As he sang he swung the club which was supposed to be his drumstick, but instead of beating the ground for rhythm he would hit a prairie dog on the head. The dancing prairie dogs did not know what was happening because their eyes were closed.

One of the prairie dogs had sore eyes and had been unable to close them entirely. When Sainday began hitting his neighbors he was, at first, too frightened to make even a faint bark. Then he got his breath and cried out, "Open your eyes! Trickster Sainday isn't using the ground as a drum; the thumping you hear is the thud of your neighbors as they fall to the ground! Uncle is hitting them on the head and killing them! Run for your holes before he kills you too!"

The startled prairie dogs opened their eyes and scampered like raining arrows in the direction of their holes. But they could not find them because crafty Sainday had plugged-up their doorways.

All the yellow prairie dogs were overtaken and killed; all the black, white, red, blue, green and purple ones were killed. All because of Sainday's mean trick. Only one pair of prairie dogs managed to escape, and they were brown. It was their hole that Sainday had missed.

Because the prairie dogs who survived were brown, all prairie dogs today are brown. There are none of a different color. Prairie dogs today wag their tails as they sit on their mounds—just as their ancestors did. And each one chatters, "Tdek-ko! Tdek-ko!" in the same manner as prairie dogs long ago. But they don't listen to strangers!

Tsai - gah, Tsai - gah! Tone - bah toe - tay.

Bah - tone toe - tay oeh - nah bah low - sa, oeh - nah bah

low - sa. Tdek-ko! Tdek-ko! Tdek-ko! Tdek-ko!

A DRUM SHOULD BEAT AT EACH QUARTER REST.

In telling this legend the Kiowa storyteller pauses to sing the prairie-dog song just as Sainday did.

Why Crows
Are Black

White Crow had never forgotten how Sainday got the buffalo back for the people when they were hungry and in need of meat and hides. Now that the people were hungry again, he felt he had managed to get his revenge. He had been warning the buffalo every time he saw a hunting party headed in their direction, and the animals would get away. White Crow would zoom down just above the herds and hiss: "Here they come. Run, run, run!"

About that time, Sainday was coming along after having been on another of his long journeys. Noticing that the villagers looked thin and sickly, he stopped at Spider Woman's lodge.

"Good day to you!" he called.

"Maybe you think it's a good day," Spider Woman replied, "but nobody in this village thinks so."

"What is the matter?"

"That White Crow is again keeping us from getting buffalo meat."

"The same as before?"

"No, but he is keeping the buffalo away somehow!"

Sainday said "Mmmm!" When he said "Mmmm!" that way, people knew he intended to do something about it. "Let me give this a good THINK."

He sat down and put his robe over his head to be alone with his thoughts. His thinking took all the rest of the morning, but by afternoon he announced that he had a plan. "I will not only see that you have plenty of meat, I'll catch White Crow and punish him so much he'll never keep the buffalo away from you again."

"How do you propose to do that?" Spider Woman asked.

"I shall turn myself into a buffalo. Remember this: when you find me with the herd, you must shoot me. Your arrows can't really touch me because I will be inside the bone. However when you are cutting off the meat be careful not to cut me. If you cut me I'll yell, and you'll be sorry because I'll turn the meat into something you can't eat.

Spider Woman and the people standing around promised to take care. Sainday went out onto the prairie and turned himself into a buffalo, something only a Trickster-Medicine person can do. He started grazing and looking for a herd of buffalo to join. Too, he was watching out of the corners of his eyes for any sight of White Crow.

Sainday didn't have long to wait for White Crow came zooming down out of the sky and alighted beside him.

"You're a stray buffalo," Crow said. "You'd better join your herd, and all of you get away from this place quickly. The hunters are getting closer every minute."

"Oh!" scoffed the buffalo-that-was-Sainday, "Those hunters wouldn't want me; my meat would be too old and tough."

"Hi-yah!" said White Crow, "That's not buffalo-talk! And your voice sounds like Sainday. Maybe you *are* Sainday!"

At that moment an arrow from a hunter's bow hit Buffalo-Sainday, and he dropped over as if dead.

He looked dead, all right, but the Sainday part of the buffalo was safe inside the bone structure of the animal.

Suspicious, White Crow hid in a clump of tall grass. He watched while the hunters took out their knives and began to skin and cut off as much meat as they could without cutting the bones. After loading the meat on a travois, they left for the village.

As soon as they were out of sight, White Crow perched on the skull of the buffalo carcass. He began pecking it hard. That hurt! Sainday could barely keep from yelling. Then White Crow hopped onto the hipbone and pecked away with all his strength. With a terrific effort Sainday held still until White Crow reached his ribs. Because Sainday was ticklish and the pecking hurt, he felt like giggling one minute and howling the next.

"If you're Sainday you won't be able to hold still now!" White Crow said and began to jump up and down and tickle the ribs more and more. That was what Sainday had been waiting for. When White Crow was in exactly the right position, Sainday closed the rib cage around Crow and held him fast. It was a trap from which he could not escape. Next, Sainday turned back into himself. There he stood with White Crow held tight in his big hands.

"You, you Trickster Sainday! I knew it was you!" White Crow yelled.

"If you knew me why did you let yourself get caught?" asked Sainday. "And don't bother to make excuses." He carried the squirming Crow to Spider Woman's tepee where she stood beside a big fire.

"Put on some green branches!" Sainday said.

Spider Woman wanted to hold White Crow to get a closer look at him. Sainday handed him over, warning her to be careful.

"So this is what he looks like!" Spider Woman said as she turned White Crow over and over. But Crow wrenched himself out of her grasp and circled above the crowd of on-lookers shouting, "Now, I'll be meaner than ever. I'll have no pity on you. I will starve the entire tribe!"

The people stared up at him and turned angrily toward Spider Woman, but then they saw that she had begun working her hands in a winding motion as if twirling a ball of twine. She was spinning a web, a spider web, that was forming around the circling White Crow. She began to pull the web toward her with the astonished Crow entangled in it.

When White Crow realized that he was again a captive, he began to plead for mercy. "Free me! I was only joking. I'll treat you kindly, if you'll let me go!" But Sainday took him from Spider Woman and ordered more green branches put on the fire.

The branches caused such dense black smoke,

the whole village came running. The smoke was soon so thick everyone began to cough.

"Let me go, Sainday!" White Crow whined. "I can hardly breathe!" His voice was a mere, feeble croak.

Sainday held White Crow in the middle of the mounting smoke, then let him go. But it was a black crow that flew away, choking and sputtering and gasping.

"You've always enjoyed impersonating a snowflake," Sainday called after him. "Now play you are smoke rising through a tepee smokehole!"

"Caw! Caw! Caw!" Crow was hardly able to speak even that much, but he did manage to add, "You—can't—do this—to me!"

"Oh yes I can!" said Sainday. "And your children and your children's children will also be the color of smoke—black, black smoke."

Spider Woman watched as the black crow vanished in the distance. "He still is as handsome as when he was white. I don't think you've punished him enough, Sainday."

"Oh have I not?" Sainday doubled-up with laughter. "Now that Crow no longer looks like a snowflake the buffalo will not be able to see him coming, nor recognize him. Besides, they will never understand him."

"Why will they not?" asked Spider Woman.

Sainday gave another of his whooping laughs.

"Crow doesn't know yet, but all he will ever be able to say is 'Caw, caw!' That smoke choked off his speaking voice."

That is why, to this day, all crows are black and the only sound they can make is a hoarse "Caw!"

Sky High
Went the Sun

In Far-Back Times one half of the world was always dark, while the other half was always full of sunshine. Finally, the people on the dark side of the world held a dance to cheer themselves up. But it didn't help. So Fox Man, Deer, and Magpie Woman sat down together on a big tree stump to try to find some way to get the sun on their side.

"It is very bad for our cornfields not to have any sun; the corn needs sun to make it grow!" Fox said.

"Our squashes and beans won't grow either," Deer agreed. "What are we going to do for food?"

"It isn't right that the people on the other side have the sun all the time," said Magpie Woman. "Let's ask Sainday to help us!"

"If we could catch Sainday in a doing-good mood, he might help us get the sun," said Deer. But if he happens to feel like playing tricks on his friends, he'd be just as likely to help those people keep the sun from us!"

Fox got up from the log and began pacing back and forth. "Sainday is like that. One never knows what to expect from him. That's why I can't keep from laughing whenever one of his tricks backfires. Do you remember when . . ." Fox didn't finish what he was about to say because a strange looking creature was coming along.

It was Sainday, but no one recognized him. His head was stuck so tightly in an old buffalo skull that he couldn't get it off without help. At first no one could make out what he was saying. When Fox, Deer, and Magpie did recognize Sainday, they just sat there laughing.

"Come now! Get this thing off my head!" Sainday begged.

"How did you get yourself in such a plight?" asked Magpie between laughs.

"I couldn't see where I was going because it was

so dark, and I fell over an old buffalo skeleton. I was trying to catch some mice I thought I heard inside the skull when my head got stuck. Get it off my head! I can hardly breathe!"

His friends stopped laughing and came to him. "Very well, Sainday. We'll get the skull off if you'll first promise that you will try to bring the sun to our side of the world."

"I'll do what I can. But that will take some THINKING, and I can't start thinking till my head is free of this thing!"

Fox, Deer, and Magpie tugged and jerked at the old skull until at last it came off. Sainday stood rubbing his neck and shaking his aching head. When he was ready to sit down to do some THINKING, he put his robe over his head to be alone with his thoughts. He did that when he needed to think.

For a long time Sainday sat without moving. Then he threw off his robe and stood up. "I'm not one to do things by halves," he said. "If you want the sun I'll get it for you and you'll have it all the time. The other side has had it long enough. This is my plan: we're going to have a relay race."

"A relay race? How will that help?" Fox asked.

"Fox, you can run the farthest without becoming winded, so you'll be first . . . ."

"But how will a relay race bring the sun to this side of the world?"

"You asked me to help you, didn't you? Just trust me."

Motioning Fox to stand beside him, he turned to Deer. "You're a good runner, too. You'll be second in the relay race. And Magpie will be third. I will be last because I'm no runner at all."

Fox grumbled under his breath, "Except when you *want* to be!"

"What's that?" Sainday said, sharply.

"Oh, I say you plan things—perfectly."

"That I do. That I do. Now Fox, you are to run to the side of the world where the sun is now and become well acquainted with the people there." Then Sainday whispered instructions in each one's ear.

"Now don't worry! We'll get the sun on our side of the world, all right!"

"Should I use my magic power to change myself from man to fox?" Fox asked.

"No, Fox Man, you can fool the Sun people better in the form of a man. And you, Deer Man, don't change yourself into a deer unless you see that we're about to lose the race. I know you run more swiftly as a deer, but still we shall win! You will see!"

In the part of the world where the sun was held, the people were playing a game of ball, and the ball was the sun. Eight players, all wearing big gloves, were lined up four to the right and four to the left. Each side had a captain, and each side had four spears, one for each player. As the players sang the Sun Game Song, the sun, a big red ball, was rolled along the ground. All players took turns throwing their spears at it. The side hitting the sun ball the most times during the length of the song was the winner. Fox, who had been nearby longer than anyone knew, slipped in and joined the many cheering spectators. He sidled up to the captain on the left side which was losing more often than the right side and said in a low voice, "Good luck to the losers!"

The captain merely glanced at Fox. When his side scored, right after that, the captain thanked Fox for wishing them luck. The left side continued winning. The players on the right side began to blame Fox for their own losses and wanted to send him away. "He doesn't belong here!" they shouted.

"No!" said the captain of the left side, "we'll not send him away!"

"I say he goes!" yelled the captain on the right side.

"He stays!"

"He goes!"

"He stays!"

Finally Fox went to the captain of the right side and told him that if he'd let him stay and join the game he'd play first on one side, then on the other and in that way would bring luck to both sides.

The captains agreed that if Fox played like that he might stay. One player was to drop out when it came Fox's turn to play on his side. Before the players returned to their game Fox said, "How do you handle that hot ball without burning your hands?" He was sly, that Fox; he had noticed their gloves, but he had his reason for asking.

The captain on the right side replied, "We have special gloves. See?" and he held up his gloved hands.

"Then how can I play on anyone's side without gloves on *my* hands?" Fox asked.

"You may use my gloves when you're playing on my side. Here," the captain said holding out his gloves, "take them now. You may have the first turn."

That was what Fox had been hoping for. He put on the gloves and took the sun ball in his hands. He bent over, as if to send it rolling along the ground. But, instead of releasing the sun ball, he started running with it.

At first all the players were too astonished to do anything but stand with their mouths and eyes wide open. So Fox got a good start. Since the light went with the sun, the people were groping in darkness by the time they realized they must chase the thief to get their sun back.

Fox ran more swiftly than he had ever run and he made good headway. The sun was getting almost too hot to hold when he saw Deer waiting to take up the relay race. Quickly he handed him the sun ball and his gloves. Deer ran and ran. He was just about to drop when he came to where Magpie was waiting. By this time the sun people had become lost in the darkness and had given up the race until they could find some way to get the sun back. Magpie didn't know that. She grabbed the sun and the gloves and ran till she reached Sainday. When he planned the relay race, Sainday hadn't been able to resist playing a little trick. He knew if all went well by the time it came his turn he wouldn't have to run at all. And that's what happened. Sainday simply flung the red sun ball over his shoulder and walked calmly along letting the people on this side of the world think he had done most of the work. The hot ball soon blistered his shoulder, and he had to put it down until his friends caught up with him.

"Now that I've brought you the sun," Sainday said, "what are you going to do with it?"

"You take care of it, Sainday. Now we'll have light to work in our gardens. And the sunshine will make things grow!" Sainday placed the big red ball in front of his tepee. He was sitting there admiring it, one day, when Fox, Deer, and Magpie came to see him.

"Now there's too much light!"

"How so?" asked Sainday.

"Things are growing too rapidly! Everything is too tall and too big around!" said Deer.

"And everything is drying out!" said Magpie. "Can't you hide the sun half the time?"

69

Sainday put the sun inside his tepee. But it kept shining through the walls and burned a hole in the top of the tepee. Next he tried hiding it under a pile of hides on his tepee floor. He sat on top to help keep the light from showing, but he didn't stay there long! With a yell he jumped up, shouting to Fox to see if his pants were smoking.

"No," said Fox, "but those hides are!" and they all rushed to save Sainday's valuable pile of hides.

"This will never do!" Sainday said. "Here, Magpie, you take the sun. I don't want it here anymore."

Magpie backed away. She didn't want it either.

"Very well," said Sainday, "here it goes!" and he tossed the sun straight up into the sky. The wind gave it a push, and the sun kept going up, up, up and never did come down.

"Now you've done it!" cried Deer. "We won't have the sun anymore!"

"But we will, it's still up there where it has room to move from one side of the world to the other. All the people can have it part of the time, now, instead of only half the people all the time."

"That's right!" shouted Fox. "It is traveling alone now, rolling toward the dark side of the world."

"Yes, and it will be back here again. You wait and see!"

And that is what happened. It's why we have night and day—because Sainday sent the sun sky high!

Masquerading Trickster

Old Man Coyote enjoyed dressing up to look like someone else. To keep his animal and people friends from knowing what he was up to he would play a masquerading game.

One sun, wanting to find out how the Crow tribesmen were getting along, Old Man Coyote set out for the village he knew so well. As he rounded a hill on the way he met a mountain goat. Before that goat knew what was happening, he found himself changed into a handsome horse with wind-tossed mane and a fat rump.

For the horse-that-was-a-goat, Old Man Coyote made an elegant saddle and bridle out of bark and a beaded saddle blanket out of leaves. With water from a rain puddle he mixed a pot of red clay and a pot of yellow clay. The yellow paint he smeared over the horse's rump, and with the red painted its ears. He then mixed juice from the purple Cone flower and used herbs of other colors to paint his own body and face.

Mounting the horse-that-was-a-goat, Old Man Coyote commanded it to prance and neigh and paw the ground the moment they reached the village.

Glancing down at his shirt that he had created out of grass and decorated with porcupine quills, and at the strings of shell beads he had made and hung about his neck, Old Man Coyote's chest stretched high with pride as he rode along. This was long and long ago before the Crow people had learned to make such fancy trappings. At that moment, Old Man Coyote became the inventor of such things.

It was almost dusk by the time Old Man Coyote entered the circle of lodges that formed the outer rim of the Crow village. Sun Chief had painted himself red and gone to his lodge in the sky just beyond the horizon.

When his horse began to neigh and paw and

prance, the people came out of their lodges to see what was happening. The handsome horse and its elegant rider made their eyes bug out and their mouths drop open. The women, especially, admired the important looking rider. Everyone began moving closer and closer. Frightened, the horse-that-was-a-goat shied away from the pressing crowd throwing Old Man Coyote off balance. Unable to keep his seat because his costume was so heavy, he tumbled to the ground with a thud that raised a big puff of dust. This frightened the horse still more, so much so, that before everyone's eyes he turned back into a mountain goat and ran away.

Now the villagers realized that Old Man Coyote had been up to his old tricks. Knowing that by touching him one could get some of his magic power, they rushed toward him. But wary Trickster quickly turned himself into a wolf and dashed away in the direction the goat had gone. As he ran his fine clothes dropped off, leaving him bare except for his breechcloth. The villagers snatched them up, only to find that they became grass, leaves, and bark in their hands.

But the men of the tribe had seen how much their women admired the elegant stranger. That is why, to this very day, Crow tribesmen put on all their finery when they want to be admired by a special person or to take part in a big powwow.

The Flowers'
Forever Land

The Ponca's Old Man Trickster was in a doing-good mood. He especially wanted to do something about the colorful flowers whose beauty was missed when they died and left the earth. So he sat down on a moss-covered log to give the matter a good THINK. He thought and he thought until he became so sleepy he tumbled off the log and just lay on the ground snoring. His noisy snoring attracted the attention of Honey-Bee who stopped on her flight to perch on Trickster's big nose. "Wake up, Old Man!" she buzzed. But Old Man Trickster only stirred a little and kept on sleeping. So Honey-Bee stung him.

"Na-na-na!" he shouted, brushing the bee from the end of his nose. "Why did you sting me?"

"I wanted you to wake up and tell me why you are here."

"I am here to do some thinking."

"Well?"

"I'm thinking about flowers."

"Oh, I'm well acquainted with flowers. I get pollen from them which allows me to make honey. Why are you thinking about them?"

"I've decided something special should be done after they die and can't help you with your honey-making nor be here for people to enjoy their color and sweet smell. Have you any suggestions?"

"No, but I'll talk with some of the flowers." Honey-Bee flew over to a bed of purple violets growing beside the trail.

Old Man sat waiting. And while he waited he applied herbs to the bee sting on his nose.

Honey-Bee flew from the violets to a clump of bluebells and from the bluebells to the sunflowers. Then she visited other flowers growing nearby— some were red, some orange, some still other colors. She visited them all.

Then she flew back to Old Man and reported,

"All the flowers want to find a home in the sky when they leave this world. They want people here to be able to see them at special times like right after a rain. Rain makes flowers grow, so they feel akin to rain."

"Fine!" Old Man replied. "Whenever the sun shines while rain is coming down we shall have something pretty to look at up there in the sky. I'll turn all dead flowers—the now-dead ones and all future ones—into a rainbow of seven colors. The violet is my favorite flower, so I'll protect all violets by putting them on the inside. Then will come the other six colors in the shape of a great arch. Does this plan please you?"

"Yes," said Honey-Bee. "I'm sorry I stung you."

"If you hadn't awakened me, I couldn't have asked you for a suggestion and you wouldn't have asked the flowers . . ." Trickster broke off and started down the trail. Turning around, he waved to Honey-Bee and called out: "Look for that rainbow next rain!"

This is how the rainbow came to be. It was one of Old Man's doing-good tricks.

Why the Buzzard's Head Is Bald

Trickster Iktoemi, who was sometimes called Grandfather because he addressed all people, animals, and birds as "Grandchild," had been traveling far and long. Four Sleeps and four Suntimes he had been away from home. His moccasins were ragged and his feet were bruised from walking over stones and stubble.

At the beginning of this fifth sun his eyes looked

like mere holes in his head; he was tired and sleepy. But he wanted to get where he was going before something happened to him. As everyone knows, everything is always done in fours, the lucky number. After that one's luck is likely to run out. For that reason when Trickster Iktoemi met a buzzard along the trail he said to him, "Grandchild, come and carry me on your back the rest of the way."

Buzzard scowled, but said, "Come on, then!"

Iktoemi straddled the big bird's back, and they soon were soaring high above the trail. "This is fine going!" shouted Iktoemi. "I'll be in the camp of the Dakotas before sundown. That's where I am headed."

"But I wasn't planning to go in that direction," Buzzard said.

"Well, you'll go that way now, or I'll kick you in the ribs," Iktoemi replied.

The wily buzzard had his own idea about that; he was remembering a time that Trickster Iktoemi had tricked him out of a good meal. Now was a chance to get revenge. He flew in a circle four times making Iktoemi so dizzy and turned around, he didn't know which way they were headed. When Iktoemi realized Buzzard had begun flying lower and lower, they were barely above the treetops. "Look out!" Grandfather shouted, "Watch yourself, Grandchild! You're likely to get us snagged on one of those branches down there!"

Buzzard made no reply so that the trickster grew more and more uneasy. When he noticed that the big bird was hovering over a hollow tree beside the dusty trail he yelled, "I command you to continue the flight to the camp of the Dakotas!"

Now Buzzard *did* reply: "Since you don't like the way I travel I'll leave you right here, Grandfather." With a swish he zoomed down and dumped Iktoemi head first into the hollow tree trunk.

Iktoemi was wedged in so tightly he could not get out; so he had to remain that way for a long, long time. His bones ached. Standing on his head didn't make breathing very easy. It was with great relief that he heard voices down below. A hunting party had set up overnight camp not far from the base of that hollow tree.

Iktoemi was wearing a raccoon skin cap with two tails on it. He poked the tails through cracks in the tree trunk, hoping, hoping that the trick he had in mind was going to work. If it didn't work, well, he knew for sure it would be his very last trick!

Women nearby caught sight of the tails waving in the wind and thought there must be two raccoons, maybe more, imprisoned in the hollow tree. Immediately they began making a hole to catch the animals.

When the hole was big enough Trickster Iktoemi came tumbling out startling the women so, that they fled without a backward look. Iktoemi hoped they would keep on going. He lay motionless, pretending to be dead. Since he was covered with raccoon skins, some of the scavenger birds began circling overhead to look him over. As he had planned they soon alighted and started pecking at him. Trickster Iktoemi lay very still, waiting for Buzzard to put in an appearance as he was sure he would. He didn't have to wait long. When Buzzard came close enough, Iktoemi jumped up and grabbed him by the neck. Buzzard struggled, but before he managed to break away, Trickster Iktoemi had torn all the feathers off the top of his head.

That is why today all buzzards are bald.

When Plum Bush
Tricked the Trickster

During a stroll along the bank of a river one sun in the Green Moons season of the year, Wihio, Old Man Trickster, stopped to rest. As he sat gazing into the water he saw some ripe plums on the bottom.

"Ummm!" he said, smacking his big lips, "I'm hungry! Those plums look so good they make my mouth water. I'm tired and hot, too. I'll dive into the river and get the plums, and I can get a bath at the same time." Wihio, Old Man Trickster, took off his clothes and dived in. He felt around for the plums, but soon had to come up for air. He couldn't hold his breath very long and the water was deep. He dived in again. No plums! Wihio climbed back up the bank and looked down in the water again. "I've made so many ripples I can't see anything down there. I'll dive a little farther to the right. Maybe that's where the plums can be found."

Four times Wihio dived in. The last time he tied a big stone around his neck to weigh him down so he could stay under water longer. The stone took him down, all right. It anchored him so that he couldn't free himself and nearly drowned. Finally, he managed to struggle free and came to the surface, gasping and sputtering. He crawled up the bank to lie exhausted on the ground.

As he lay on his back, looking up at the turquoise blue sky he was glad he hadn't drowned. Yet he was angry because he had not found the plums. Turning his head his squinty eyes lighted on something—above him was a plum tree full of fruit. He sat up with a jerk and looked over his shoulder to make sure no one had come along and witnessed all this. Now he knew that the plums he had seen in the water were only a reflection of the plums on that tree. The ripples had smoothed out and again he could see the plums on the mirror-like surface of the river.

There was one thing sure: The plum tree had tricked old Trickster!

Story of the End
of Trickster Wihio

One sun when Old Man Wihio was coming along he came upon a man living all alone who had a great amount of meat drying on racks or hanging upon branches beside his tepee. Trickster Wihio greeted the man and remarked on his piles of hides and furs. The man, who was cooking some meat, invited Wihio to have supper with him.

While they were eating tasty meat stew and roasted ears of corn, Wihio noticed a huge sack of something tied to the center lodgepole. The more he looked at it, the more his curiosity grew.

As night spread a dark blanket over the earth he said to the man, "I am too weary to travel farther tonight. How about letting me sleep here in your lodge?"

Wihio only pretended to sleep. He lay there waiting for his host to start snoring. When the man's snoring became long and loud Old Man Trickster got up and untied the sack from the lodgepole.

With the sack flung over his shoulder he slipped out of the tepee and hurried away. Soon he came to a lake which, in the darkness, he mistook for a river. He started running along the bank hoping to put quite a distance between himself and his sleeping host before the man should awake and miss his sack.

Wihio didn't know he was going round and round the shore of a lake. It seemed to him that the "river" had no end. The sack was heavy, too. He became so weary he decided to crawl up on the bank and rest awhile.

When Sun Chief arose and painted himself at the east horizon, the man in the tepee awoke and immediately missed his guest and the sack from his lodgepole. Rushing outside he stumbled over Wihio lying asleep not far from the tepee with his head resting on the missing sack. Wihio was startled to find he was back at the man's lodge.

The man shouted at him, "Now what are you doing with my sack?"

"Oh!" Wihio tried to look as if he had had the best of intentions. "Well, you see it was this way, my brother. You have treated me so well, I was intending to offer to carry your sack for you when you move."

"When I move? Who said I was going to move?" the man jerked the sack from under Wihio's head and hung it back in its place on the lodgepole.

Wihio said, "My brother, I can see that you are afraid of something. What is it? I have some magic power, and maybe I can help you."

"Well, I fear nothing at all . . . except . . ."

"Except what?"

"Except a goose."

"A goose! Well! Strange that you should say that because that's the one thing I can't help you with. I, too, am afraid of a goose. A goose is a dangerous fowl to some people." Then Wihio stood up and told the man goodbye.

That night Wihio changed himself into the form of a goose and returned to the man's lodge. Behind it he made loud noises like an angry goose. This frightened the man so much he grabbed his sack and ran out of the lodge with it. He kept on running and soon disappeared in the darkness. Wihio bent over with laughter at the success of his trick.

When morning came Wihio followed the man's tracks till he discovered where he had gone. The man had built himself a little brush shelter where he was keeping a tight hold on his sack. Wihio hid from him till dark. Then he sneaked up and again made angry goose noises. The man was more frightened than before. He ran outside and kept running as long as his legs held up. He still had the sack with him.

A third and a fourth time Wihio frightened the man with his honking, cackling, and hissing noises. Four times the man ran, carrying the sack with him. The fifth time, Wihio let the man see the "goose" as well as hear it. This time the man was shaking with such fear that he dropped the sack on the ground and dared not return for it.

Although he had gained success on the *fifth* try, Wihio feared to press his luck any farther, so he did not follow the man to make sure he would not return for his sack. However, the frightened man was going so fast Wihio was sure he would never see him again. He changed back to himself and returned to the man's lodge where he opened the sack.

To his amazement a cow buffalo jumped out. In the sack Wihio saw heads of other buffalo crowding toward the opening. He quickly closed the sack and hung it in its usual place. He killed the buffalo and had food for a very long time.

When all the meat was gone Wihio opened the sack again, and another buffalo jumped out. He tied the sack and hung it up. When that meat was gone he did the same thing again. And still another time. This made the *fourth* time.

Now Wihio was well aware that it is safe to do certain things four times but unsafe to do them a fifth time. He always had a hard time keeping track of the number of times and often got into trouble as a result. Now was one of those times when he had completely lost count, and the moment he opened the sack a buffalo bull rushed out, and Wihio could not close the sack. Many more buffalo rushed out. Bellowing and pawing the ground, the big animals knocked Old Man Wihio down and trampled him until he begged them to stop and listen to him. Shouting to be heard, he promised never again to play tricks on the Cheyenne people.

As the chief of the Buffaloes listened shaking his massive head from side to side, Trickster shouted promises and rubbed his aching body. Finally Buffalo Chief said, "Very well, but you had better keep your promise!" Then he motioned for the herds to fan out all over the plains and hills. They ran north, south, east, and west. That is how the buffalo came into this world.

That also is why Trickster, Old Man Wihio, went *out* of this world. He decided he had done enough trickery and enough good deeds to last everybody a lifetime and had better stop "coming along" as Buffalo Chief had warned him. OR ELSE!

He told all the birds and animals and trees and shrubs and the Cheyenne people goodbye. To the Cheyennes this was the end of Old Man Trickster, otherwise known as Wihio.

Postword

Members of numerous tribes generally agree that when Trickster—by whatever name—was about to leave this world he raised his right arm and spread out his fingers in a dramatic gesture and said to the animals, birds, trees, and people, "Up there in the big Sky World is where I am going, but in the daytime while you're working I will be keeping an eye on all of you down here. I'll keep an ear open,

too. If you ever tell stories or make jokes about me in the daytime, I'll hear you, and I won't like it. At night while I am sleeping, you may talk about me all you please. But not in the daytime. Remember that!"

Trickster yawned and stretched himself, then turned to go. He stopped and looked back at them from across his left shoulder. "If you should forget my warning—and I mean you—and you—and you—" He pointed his bony forefinger in all directions, "You'll be sorry when I come back and cut off the end of your nose!" Then he made himself disappear from sight.

And so the general conclusion of all tribespeople is: THAT'S THE WAY IT WAS—AND IS—DOWN TO THIS VERY DAY.